Grandma's Christmas Wish

by
Shelley Bingham Husk

Leicester Bay
B O O K S

Newport, Maine

First Edition(CS) – First Printing
ISBN-13: 978-0692735084 (Leicester Bay Books)
ISBN-10: 0692735089
Kindle Edition: 2016

Leicester Bay Books
P.O. Box 536
Newport ME 04953-0536

www.leicesterbaybooks.com

Contents

Acknowledgements

Nearly all of the anecdotes told in this book are true accounts from family members. My father, Loran Bingham, shot the neighbor girl with the BB gun through a hole in the outhouse when he was 5, and when we were growing up, each year he would bring home a Christmas tree that was too big and had to be cut to fit into the living room. My step-mother, VerDaun Bingham, still wears one-legged hose, marks old cottage cheese containers for re-use, and proudly displays the Christmas mouse, she made at church in the 1980's, every year. My mother, Mary Faun Chauvie, adored chocolate covered cherries and hung baggies over the sink to dry for re-use. Lying on her death bed, My Grandmother Arita Bingham, told her dead sister to send my grandfather, Loran Bingham, back to get her or she wasn't going anywhere. And my brother, Craig, at two years old, wearing only a diaper, climbed up the Christmas tree and slid down, taking many branches with him.

Dedication

To family, past, present and future, who willingly share their stories, in spite of the embarrassment they may cause. Because truly, you can't make this stuff up!

CHAPTER ONE
Kate Reilly

KATE REILLY SAT ACROSS THE DESK from her trusted lawyer and friend, Martin Westerly. She was the epitome of an old-world Irish woman, stout and stubborn, with an air of sadness about her. Martin Westerly was the exact opposite, nice-looking, well-spoken and always smiling. Although they were nearly the same age, Kate Reilly's life had taken a toll that made her appear more as Martin's mother than his peer.

This particular morning, Kate was not at Martin's office for a visit. Her reasons were much more pressing. "If all else fails," Kate said, "Maybe they'll come home for my funeral."

Martin interrupted, "Kate Reilly, you know your grandkids love you."

"Darby, yes, of course, I raised her. But Jack doesn't come around anymore and I haven't seen Claire in, I don't know how long."

"You know Kate," Martin said, "Jack. Well, Jack's just Jack. And Claire doesn't know the whole truth – "

"And she never will. It's okay Martin. Let's just get this Will in order. I think I may need it sooner than later."

"Now, Kate Reilly, don't you go getting all hopeless on me. You know what the doctor said."

"Hope springs eternal." Kate let out a slight chuckle. "But I'm no spring chicken and eternity's looking pretty good right now."

Martin and Kate had been friends since the day she and her husband John came to town. The three of them had a bond like that of siblings. They supported and backed each other up, no matter what the obstacle. And there were many. Martin had no children and when his wife, Violet fought and lost her twenty year bout with cancer, the Reilly's were there to help Violet die and Martin live again.

Kate looked down at the papers she was about to sign. She thought back to a happier time. Not necessarily an easier time, just happier. "Do you remember when the kids were all teeny?" She asked. "We used to tie a bunch of inner tubes together and float down Big Wood River?"

"I do." Martin answered. "It seems like three lifetimes ago."

Then Kate thought back even farther. "You know, I was only 17 when I married John Reilly.

"I know."

"We came to America with very little money and a few pieces of Irish crystal that John's parents gave us as a wedding present."

"Yes," Martin said, humoring Kate. He had heard the story many times before. But now, it seemed to him as though Kate needed to tell the story. As if it would be her last time to recall, that soon after she and John Reilly married, they left Ireland and set sail for America.

The voyage to America was difficult because they had to travel in the steerage section of the boat. Many people got sick and some even died, as the conditions were deplorable, with the boat rocking the filth back and forth like a muddy tide slapping at the shore.

The crystal John and Kate brought with them was stunning. When the light hit it just right, it was as if stars were dancing just for them. But it had to be hidden while on the boat, for fear that it would be stolen. No matter how hard times got, they would save the crystal for their infant daughter, Madison Jean.

But, Madison Jean was one of the casualties of the disease ridden boat. John and Kate's baby girl did not survive the passage from Ireland to America. "I held Maddie in my arms as she slipped away and there was nothing I could do to save her. I would have happily jumped into the ocean that day and let God take me home to be with my little girl. But John, my sweet John, he gave me hope," Kate said.

"John was a good man," Martin added.

"We got to this town with nothing, except the crystal. I would have traded all of it to be carrying my baby into our new home instead of a handful of useless things."

"But you're a survivor."

Kate's way of surviving was to immerse herself in work. The sadder she got, the harder she worked. She and John opened the town's first general store and she spent every spare moment there.

John & Kate became very successful.

Eventually, they added a lumber mill to the Reilly holdings. It was the largest building in town, towering above the others like the sun overlooking a garden.

Kate and John Reilly had the best that life could offer. They built a massive house on the outskirts of town. It really was a mansion, but they never called it that. To them, it was home. The Reilly house stood proudly in the front of five acres of property, like it was part of a horizon that God Himself had created.

A pond with ducks, sat at one end of the property and a chicken coop at the other. In the mornings, you could hear the chatter back and forth, as if the birds were neighbors gossiping in the yard. Completing the pastoral view was a large greenhouse and two Appaloosa horses. No cows. The coats on the horses mimicked that of a spotted cow and that would have to suffice.

It seemed to the outside world that John and Kate Reilly had everything. But they could not have a child.

The days turned into years and the one thing their money could not buy was a child. All they wanted was to bless someone else with all that their love and money could give. So, Kate's kitchen door was always opened to everyone. Children and adults alike would stop by for good food and conversation. Kate would take the young ones out to feed the ducks in the pond. The horses were available for anyone who wanted to ride them. There was no shortage of kids playing on the Reilly property. But something was still missing.

Many years passed, and by some miracle Kate became pregnant. At an early doctor's appointment, she was told, it would be dangerous for her to have the baby. The baby she had longed for could kill her.

Kate prayed and prayed. She spent so much time on her knees, they looked more like eggplants than knees. She was a strong Christian and believed God would answer her prayers. So, against her doctor's advice, Kate kept her baby. She stayed in bed for nearly seven months growing this tiny human being. Finally, after what seemed like an eternity, God sent Kate and John another daughter, Hannah Reilly.

Hannah married Danny Cavanaugh and together they had three children, Claire, Jack and Darby. The universe smiled on the Reilly family. That is, until the fatal car accident that killed Kate's only daughter and son-in-law, along with her beloved husband, John Reilly. In her unimaginable grief, Kate Reilly was left to take care of her three grandchildren.

Now, many years later, it was her last wish that they be a family again.

CHAPTER TWO
Bill Simons

MARTIN WESTERLY was not only the most prominent attorney in town–he was the only attorney in town. His office sat smack in the middle of the little block of buildings that comprised Main Street. No matter where you were coming from or going to, the distance was pretty much the same to Martin's office.

This particular day, Martin sat across the desk from Bill Simons, a self-made-dot-com multi-millionaire. At one time Bill was a beautiful man inside and out. But something had soured him. The mood was quite different from when Kate Reilly was there weeks earlier.

Bill didn't waste any time, he chimed right up, "I have no desire to let this opportunity go. I've worked too hard."

"Would you be doing this if Claire hadn't run off?" Martin asked.

"Leave Claire out of this Martin, this is just business."

"Do you realize what your "business" is going to do to the Reilly family, this town – to Claire?"

Bill could not be swayed. "Look Martin, when the economy went downhill, I was there for Kate Reilly. She was completely lucid when she signed the note.

"I'm not disputing that the note is legal"

"I'm sorry she's ill. But I'm a businessman, not a charity worker.

"Businessman? Come on Bill, you play with computers all day."

"You call it playing with computers, I call it making millions."

"Right. And you have enough money to last you three lifetimes. What do you really want with Reilly, Inc?"

"It's not about the money," Bill insisted. "Right is right."

"Right?" Martin asked. "Isn't that why you lent Kate the money in the first place?"

Bill paused for a moment. And for that moment, Martin thought he had gotten through. But Bill was done debating. "The paperwork stipulates the first of the year. That's how long they've got."

"What if –"

"There is no what if. They have until January first,

and then I'm taking the store, the past due loans, the house, all of it!"

Martin pleaded, "Maybe if you understood, you wouldn't be so hard on the family."

"For a long time," Bill said, "all I understood was that without so much as a phone call, Claire ran off with my best friend."

"That was a long time ago and I know she had her reasons," Martin said.

"That's great," Bill replied. "She had her reasons. And now, I have mine. They have until the first of the year."

"Give the kids a chance. They'll be here. Come on Bill, they just lost they're grandmother."

"Claire'll be home for the funeral?"

"The kids are coming home for the reading of the Will."

"Will?" Bill asked.

"It's what Kate wanted"

"So Jack and Claire are coming home?"

"Yes," Martin said. "Wouldn't it bother you to run into Claire in view of what you're planning to do to the family?"

"Why should it? I may run into my old best friend as well."

"Not likely, since they're no longer married."

The news that Claire was no longer married, was a shock to Bill Simons, but the wheels were already set in motion, and unless something drastic were to happen, he would soon be the owner of Reilly, Inc.

CHAPTER THREE
Jack, Darby and Claire

ON THE VERGE OF CHANGING STATUS from that of a collector, to that of a hoarder, twenty-seven-year-old Jack Cavanaugh sat at his desk in a small, extremely cluttered loft in Los Angeles, California. Surrounded by stack after stack of books; a rather eclectic array of furniture; art pieces, framed and unframed, were lined up in almost neat rows which obstructed passage to anywhere in the room without a considerable detour, Jack finally found the phone buried between a first edition of "The American" by Henry James and a signed Winslow Homer painting.

Jack's phone rang, and as soon as he was able to unbury it, he answered, "This is Jack."

Jack's sister Darby was on the other end. She spent the better part of ten minutes explaining to Jack that their grandma, Kate had died and he was needed at home.

It was obvious by the mess in Jack's apartment that he

was swamped, but there really was no excuse good enough to keep him from going home for a few days, so he gave in. The only thing putting a damper on Darby's excitement that her brother was coming home, was the fact that she had to call her older sister Claire and convince her to come home as well.

Darby sat in her room, looking around at the pictures of her and her grandmother. To Darby, Grandma was the most beautiful woman on earth. But Claire didn't feel the same. Claire only knew the hard, bitter old woman who needed order and didn't tolerate chaos. Darby knew Grandma. She knew the hardships she had overcome to make a life for her family. She knew how the loss of both of her daughters and her husband had caused a cavernous sadness that could not be filled.

Darby looked at the pictures of her parents and siblings. But they weren't at all recent. Darby had grown up since those pictures were taken, and even more since her sister saw her last. She contemplated how she would tell Claire that she was needed at home. She was pretty sure Claire wouldn't care, and even more certain that she would not want to come home.

And she was right.

Claire had eloped and left Idaho with Blake "Johnny"

Johnson at age nineteen. Not so much because she loved him, but because he was her way out. She blamed her grandmother for the death of her parents and couldn't wait to get out of that house. Since Johnny promised to take Claire far away from the small Idaho town she had grown to hate, he was able to whisk her away before she had time to tell anyone. Including her boyfriend, Bill Simons.

Johnny was a stockbroker on Wall Street, so he and Claire lived in a great house just outside of New York City, with name brand everything, including a pure-bred dog, bought to replace any thoughts Claire might have of bringing children into the perfect life that Johnny had forged for them.

Claire was a corporate attorney and when the economy went south, Johnny decided to quit Wall Street and try his hand at his life-long dream of acting, leaving Claire to support their posh lifestyle.

Darby reluctantly called Claire. Talking to her, she felt like that little girl from so many years ago, pleading with her big sister to take her to feed the ducks.

Claire surveyed all the things that she had accumulated in nearly ten years of marriage to Johnny. Although the house was filled with beautiful expensive things, she felt empty inside. In that instant, she realized that too much time had passed since she had seen her sister and brother. Even though it meant going back to her grandmother's house, Claire would go home.

Darby hung up the phone and twirled around like a little child, dizzily recalling the last time the family had all been together. Her excitement was palpable, after nearly a decade, the three Cavanaugh children would be reunited.

CHAPTER FOUR

The Homecoming

IT WAS A COUPLE OF DAYS LATER. Darby had spent the entire morning getting ready to see the brother and sister she had not seen in many years. She cooked and cleaned and cooked some more. The fridge was filled with all manner of food. Tuna casserole, spaghetti, apple pie, homemade whipped cream and any other food she remembered her siblings liking. In between bouts of domestication, she spent much of the day, like a child waiting for the ice cream man, spying out the family room window.

Finally, a taxi pulled into the driveway. Darby ran out to see who it was. The door opened and out came her brother. Darby ran and jumped into his arms, "Jack!"

"Look at you, Noodle," he said. "You sure aren't a noodle anymore. You finally filled out, huh?"

Darby was a little embarrassed. Since Jack had last

seen her, she had become quite curvy.

"Sorry Noodle, didn't mean to make you uncomfortable." So not to further humiliate his sister, Jack changed the subject. "Is there any food inside?" He asked.

"Is this the Reilly house?" Darby answered.

With that, Jack and Darby went inside. Jack felt uneasy as he entered the house, like old ghosts from the past were still lingering.

CHAPTER FIVE
Claire's Reluctance

UNLIKE JACK, Claire wasn't so eager to return to the home she ran away from many years earlier. She pulled into the driveway in a sports car that was so shiny red, you almost wanted to lick it.

Claire got out of her car, with her suitcase, and walked straight to the greenhouse – Claire's sanctuary. She used to sit amongst the herbs and flowers and ponder for hours. This time, after a few minutes, she got up and walked slowly back to the house. She opened the door and called out, "Anybody here?" Then under her breath she continued, "In this miserable old house."

The house was just the way Claire remembered it. Very big and very full of antiques and collectables. Pretty much all that the 'American Dream' could afford the Reilly's. The carpets were hand woven and every wall was adorned with fine art, chair rails and window coverings. It was all a bit much for Claire. *This seems excessive, even for me—and that's saying something*, she thought.

Jack and Darby ran to meet Claire. It was obvious to them that another ten years would not have been long enough for Claire to feel comfortable in the Reilly house.

Darby called out Claire's name as she ran to hug her.

Jack could see Claire's discomfort and tried to lighten the mood. He smacked her on the shoulder and said, "Hey Sis, it's good to see you. I wasn't sure you'd come."

"I wasn't sure either," Claire acknowledged. "Not sure why I came. It's against my better judgment."

Darby, clung to her big sister, "I hope it was me," she said. "But, whatever the reason, I'm glad you're here."

"Where's that husband of yours?" Jack asked.

Claire was not ready to tell her sister and brother that she was divorced. She felt like she didn't know them well enough anymore. Too much time had passed. "He had to work," she said.

"Bummer." Jack said, "I would have liked to see him."

"I'm sure. How about you show me where I'm sleeping? The sooner we can get this over with, the sooner I can get out of here."

Darby grabbed Claire and Jack by the hands. She was so excited to have everyone together again. "Your rooms are ready," she said.

"Ready?" Jack asked.

As they started heading up the stairs, Claire pulled away. "I don't know if I can do this."

"Grandma's gone now," Darby said, "Whatever problems you had died with her."

Jack joined in, "Come on sis, I haven't seen you in forever. Just come check out your room."

As they went upstairs, memories flooded Claire's mind. She could see her mother singing Darby to sleep; could hear everyone laughing throughout the house. Every vase, every piece of furniture, every lamp was exactly where she remembered it being when she left home.

Jack went straight to his old room and Darby continued on with Claire.

Claire walked into her room and could not believe it. Just like the rest of the house, her room had been preserved exactly how it was when she left. Her vanity still had the old perfume bottles and lotions sitting on it; her hair brush, and some old make-up were there as well. Her cheerleader pom-poms and trophies were proudly displayed and dusted as if they had just been placed there.

Jack came running into the room. "It's like stepping into a time warp, huh Sis?"

Claire didn't think it was that cool at all. "Yeah, it's

kind of creepy–so long ago." She examined her high school bedding and continued, "So much for the past staying in the past."

"She always hoped you'd come back," Darby said. "She was never quite the same after you left. She felt so–"

"So guilty?" Claire asked. She was triggered now and the last thing Darby wanted was for her sister to be upset.

"I was going to say, sad." That seemed to set Claire off. "Sad? I hope she was sad. She killed our parents."

"Whoa" Jack said, "Don't you think that's a little harsh?"

"I don't know Jack, is it?" Claire was speaking out of anger now. "You were pretty quick to get out of here."

"That's not fair. You know I had a job I couldn't turn down."

"A Masters in Computer Graphics and you took a job driving a truck. That would be hard to turn down," Claire said sarcastically.

Darby, always the peacemaker, the one who didn't make waves, was not sure how to make the situation okay. Or maybe she did. "There are plenty of other rooms, if this one bothers you," she said. "Can't we just try?"

Jack could see that Darby, in her childlike way, was trying to fix a problem that was much too big for her to handle. So, he did what any good brother would do under the circumstances, he changed the subject. "Hey, I'm starving. Let's say we call a truce and go raid the kitchen. Come on, Sis, I heard from a reliable source that the Reilly kitchen is still stocked to the gills."

Claire was still triggered. She had no idea returning to the old house would have such an effect on her. "I'm not hungry," she said.

"Come on, Claire," Darby pleaded. "There's tons of food in the fridge. I cooked your favorite. Spaghetti with giant meatballs."

"That's one thing that was never lacking in this house," Jack said, as he started towards the kitchen.

"Yeah, the one thing," Claire mumbled.

CHAPTER SIX
Plastic-Ware Wars

CLAIRE WALKED SLOWLY into the old kitchen. Once more the memories flooded her mind, and again, she pushed them away. She thought that if she remembered good times with Grandma and the rest of the family, her reasons for leaving so long ago may not stand up as having been justified. Even by her own intense scrutiny.

Jack and Darby rummaged through the fridge, while Claire stood off to the side. Jack found an old cottage cheese container on one of the shelves. On the lid were seven different dates written in marker and scribbled out to show the latest use, and in spite of Claire's decision to neither eat nor have fun, the reminiscing began.

Of course, Jack started it. Jack always started it. "Oh wow, look they're still here. Remember, the plastic-ware wars?" he asked. He got so excited, he picked up a dishcloth and placed it over his head like a bonnet and commenced the perfect imitation of a conversation between his Grandma and Grandpa Reilly.

"Katie, do you think we could use the new containers I bought you?"

"John, The one's we have will do just fine."

Before long Darby was joining in, "Oh yeah, then Grandpa would get all hurt and start mumbling."

Jack couldn't resist but to continue the imitation, "I don't see the point of having such nice things if they're going to sit in the cupboard collecting dust."

By now, Darby and Jack were laughing out loud.

"I half expected to see the untouched box of plastic containers still sitting in the cupboard. Whatever happened to them?" Jack asked.

Darby explained that, after Claire left Grandma gave the good plastic-ware to a women's shelter. Claire was shocked to hear that her grandmother had a soft side. As Darby described her funny, kind and generous grandma, Claire felt like she was talking about someone else.

"This is too much for one night," Claire said. "I'm going to bed."

Claire headed off while Jack and Darby created a feast.

"I hope Claire's gonna be okay," Darby added.

"She'll be fine."

"I guess," Darby said. "You about done. I'm exhausted."

"What? Am I the only fun one left in this family?"

"Of course you are," Darby said tossing a blueberry at Jack. "Turn the light out when you're done stuffing your face."

Darby gave Jack a big hug and headed to her room.

CHAPTER SEVEN
Grandma's Pancakes

THE NEXT MORNING, Claire and Jack woke up to the sound of rustling coming from the kitchen and the delicious and distantly familiar smell of food. They met in the hall. Claire seemed better. "Smells like pancakes," she exclaimed.

Food was always a positive thing in the Reilly house. "And bacon," Jack replied. "Race ya!" He pushed Claire out of the way and began to run down the stairs, like it was Christmas morning. Claire followed behind.

As they entered the kitchen, Jack declared his victory, "Ha!"

Claire was unimpressed. She looked at Jack with indifference and said, "Easy to win, when you're the only one racing."

"Kill joy." Jack said, as he grabbed a plate and started piling on the pancakes.

Darby looked up from the stove, "Hungry much?"

"Only always," Jack grabbed another pancake with his hand.

Darby smacked Jack's hand. "Mind your manners, young man."

Claire took a moment and looked at Darby and Jack. "Look how you guys have changed."

"You mean got old," Darby said, looking at Jack.

Jack smacked Darby and started to butter his pancakes. "Are these Grandma's buttermilk pancakes?" he asked.

"Yep, she taught me how to make them years ago." Jack continued to chow down and Darby continued, "How about you start on the dishes, big brother?"

"I'm not the only one here, Noodle."

Darby grabbed the plate of bacon. "You keep talking, brother, I'll just eat all these myself."

With that Jack tried to take a piece of bacon, but Darby thwarted his advances with a set of tongs, reminiscent of when Grandma used to try to keep Jack away from the food before it was ready.

"Do you really think we'll run out?" Jack asked.

"It's possible, with you around," Darby replied. "Make you a deal, all the bacon you can eat, or what's on the plate, whichever comes first, and then dishes."

Jack didn't concede. He grabbed a piece of bacon and started to eat. As he was eating, he caught a glimpse of Claire nibbling on an unbuttered, dry pancake and said, "My goodness, Claire, look how beautiful you are."

After living in the shadows of her narcissist husband for years, Claire was less than convinced of her beauty. At the very least, she did not handle compliments very well. Her reaction was to look away and pretend she didn't hear the nice remarks Jack made. He continued. "Are we gonna be seeing babies from you and Johnny any time?"

It didn't take long for both Darby and Jack to see that this hit a nerve. So Darby jumped in, "What's up?"

The usually outspoken, strong Claire was reduced to a mumble. "Johnny always thought kids would be too complicated."

Darby started to rant, "Too complicated! What kind of bull is that?"

"Besides," Claire said. "I have a dog and my work. That keeps me busy enough for now."

Lucky for all involved, Martin Westerly walked in through the outside kitchen door.

"Good," Martin exclaimed. "You're all here. Jack, Claire, glad you could make it."

The kids loved Martin. He had always been a great friend of the family. They hugged him and welcomed him into the house. Martin kissed Darby on the cheek and whispered, "I need to see you privately after the services."

Although Jack and Claire hadn't been around for years, they felt a bit slighted by Martin's attention to Darby. But they forgot all about it when Martin announced, "The funeral is this afternoon."

"This afternoon," Claire said.

Jack followed with, "Why so soon?"

"Tuesday's Christmas Eve. Darby and I thought it best if we moved it up so you could have the rest of the weekend to yourselves."

"Oh, Darby thought, did she?" Claire said.

"I won't be able to schedule the reading of the will until next week." Martin continued, "That ought to give you kids a few days to catch up."

Darby pleaded with her brother and sister to stay.

Darby's petition seemed to work on Jack. He never could resist her pouty little face. Even though she wasn't so little anymore. "Okay," Jack said, stealing a pancake off of Darby's plate. She tried to stab him with her fork, but missed. "Besides, it'll be good to spend some time with my sibs."

Darby flipped a pancake onto her plate and gave Jack a smirk before working on Claire, "Can we spend Christmas together, please, Sis? You know, like Grandma's wish."

Jack and Claire didn't know what Darby was talking about. It had been too long since Grandma's wish had been spoken. So Darby explained, "You remember when we were younger, every year we'd ask her what she wanted for Christmas and she'd always say –"

Claire remembered, and sarcastically continued, "My only wish for Christmas is to have my family gathered around me."

Darby was glad that Claire remembered, until she continued, "Yet another one of Grandma's ways to control everyone."

Jack saw the dejected look on Darby's face and reacted with, "Wow, Claire."

"Fine, I'll stay. Not like I have a choice," Claire relented.

Martin saved the moment by speaking up, "So, it's settled then. I'll be back here Monday morning at 9:00 am. We can meet in the library."

Darby was so excited, she flipped another pancake just as Martin picked up a plate. The pancake landed smack in the middle of his plate, with a little help from Martin. "Nice toss, Darby," he said. "So, how are Grandma's world famous pancakes this morning?"

Jack pushed towards Darby to get to the stove again,

but Darby purposely skipped him and placed the rest of the fresh stack of pancakes on Martin's plate. "Not as good as Grandma makes them, but they'll do in a pinch."

Jack wrapped a pancake around a piece of bacon and inhaled it. "No complaints here."

The talk, teasing and eating continued for a while. Darby had created a spread that any hotel would be proud to serve for their morning buffet. It made her happy to cook. Especially for the people she loved.

Sometimes Darby would cook for days before writing a new story. Somehow cooking cleared her mind to make room for her imagination.

Each of the Cavanaugh children had their way of calming stress and clearing their minds. Darby had her writing, Jack had his computers, and Claire had her greenhouse.

CHAPTER EIGHT
The Greenhouse

AFTER BREAKFAST, Claire walked out to her greenhouse, while Jack and Darby stayed behind to finish cleaning up. That was Claire's way.

As she studied the variety of herbs, she remembered the time she had spent there, in solitude. She would sit for hours on a small old wooden bench that since then had aged as she did, and was no longer sturdy enough to sit on. Remarkably, the bench was still there amongst the lavender and rosemary. Claire ran her hands across the rough weathered wood.

Jack quietly came to the opening of the greenhouse. He did not want to interrupt Claire. It was common for her to spend half of the day amongst the foliage that lived inside. He quietly knocked on a piece of metal that was used to build the greenhouse, and waited for an invitation to enter. Claire was so engulfed in thought, that she didn't mind when he came in and stood a couple feet from her.

"I used to love it here," Claire said, smelling the herbs and pinching leaves off to sample as she passed each row.

Jack closed the gap between them. "I remember you would never let us intrude when you were in here contemplating life."

"Things change."

"Is everything okay, Claire, you seem so unhappy?"

"Like I said, things change."

"What things?"

Just as the conversation between Jack and Claire was getting a bit philosophical, Darby bounced in all happy and Claire didn't want to bring Darby down. "I'm fine," Claire said.

Darby was completely oblivious to the fact that Claire was not herself. How would she know what Claire's 'self' was. She hadn't seen her since she was a little girl. "Isn't it beautiful, Claire? We still use fresh herbs in everything."

"I could tell. You're quite the cook, Darby"

"Speaking of cooking," Jack said. "Isn't it lunch time? You've been out here forever."

"It's funeral time," Darby said. "Lunch here, after."

"Your stomach is amazing," Claire said. "Does it do any other tricks besides tell time?"

"Hysterical," Jack said, Tapping Claire on the

shoulder as if he were starting a game of tag.

Jack, Claire and Darby ran from the greenhouse to the back door of the kitchen as fast as they could. Even Claire was trying hard to keep up.

CHAPTER NINE
The Funeral

SOME PEOPLE BELIEVE God smiles on funerals for the good ones. Kate Reilly was one of the good ones. It was a beautiful winter day at the cemetery. Mourners of every age, shape, size and occupation crowded around at the gravesite. In fact, it turned out to be a good thing no one else in town died at the same time, because everyone was at Kate Reilly's funeral.

When the preacher began the sermon, they could hear a pin drop, all except for the Cavanaugh children. They had questions. They had lots of questions.

"Why did Grandma have a closed casket?" Jack asked.

"Grandma wanted to be remembered in life, not as a shell in a casket," Darby replied.

That made Jack a little sad. "I would liked to have

seen her one last time," Jack said.

Claire was mystified at her unfamiliarity with the Grandma everyone else around her seemed to love. She felt slighted, like everyone else got the good Grandma and she got the mean Grandma. "Evidently she was two different people," Claire said.

"Well, I knew both grandmas and she would want us celebrating, not thinking about some cold, white, shell in a casket. Grandma always said, 'Death is just the next step towards perfection.'"

At that point, the preacher wrapped up his sermon and the kids each placed a flower on the casket. While this was going on, Bill Simons was leaning up against his car, watching Claire from a distance.

Darby said, "She's with Grandpa and Mom now."

"And Dad," Claire said.

Bill got in his car and drove away before anyone noticed him. The mourners filed out of the cemetery and headed to the Reilly mansion. It was the longest procession in the town's history.

Everyone loved Kate Reilly.

Mourners from the cemetery filed into the house, carrying casseroles, desserts, and other food for a late lunch. Claire, Jack and Darby were there to greet them.

AFTER A FEW HOURS and many stories, the Cavanaugh kids said goodbye to the last of the guests as they trickled out of the house. It had been a long day and they were exhausted. Martin Westerly was the last to go. He hugged Claire and Jack and as he walked to the door, he whispered something in Darby's ear and walked out the door.

"What did he say?" Jack asked.

"Nothing," Darby said, and she quickly changed the subject. "How about we see what's left in the kitchen?" She asked.

Jack was all over it. He could never turn down food. "I'm up for that," he said. "I think my stomach's about to eat a hole through my shirt."

"You must have a hollow leg," Darby said, as she and Jack rifled through the mountain of the leftover food.

Claire picked up a dish rag and began to wipe the already clean tile counters. She kept on cleaning. In spite of requests from Jack and Darby for her to stop and eat, Claire would not. It was a nervous, sort of agitated cleaning. Like if she stopped wiping the tiles, her life would crumble on the spot. "I'm not really hungry," she said.

"You know turning down food in the Reilly kitchen is heresy," Jack said.

"Leave her alone, or I'll reacquaint you with the wooden spoon," Darby said. "You remember the wooden spoon, don't you Jack?"

Jack laughed, "Oh, I remember the wooden spoon."

"You ought to," Claire said. "You saw it more than anyone else in this house."

"Had a close personal relationship, if memory serves," Darby said.

"All right, all right, very funny," Jack replied.

"Well, I'm off to bed," Darby announced, passing out hugs. "I've got church in the morning. Anybody wanna go with?"

"Not me," Claire said. "I stopped believing in God when our parents were killed."

"My gosh, Claire," Darby said. "It was an accident! God didn't make it happen"

"You're right there. If Grandmother hadn't chased them out of the house..."

Jack finally stepped in. "I was there and I don't remember her chasing anyone," he said.

"Sure, take her side. I know what I saw. My parents are dead because your grandmother couldn't keep her mouth shut!"

"You don't know everything," Darby explained. "Grandma lost her only child and husband that night. He was the love of her life."

Claire wasn't ready to hear any of it. She slammed a plate down on the counter. "Don't expect me to feel sorry for her. And don't expect me to go to your church! God may not have caused it, but He could have stopped it!" she yelled, storming out of the room.

Darby and Jack could hear her footsteps all the way to her bedroom.

Jack could see that Darby was very upset. She was so young when her parents died and she didn't fully understand Claire's anger. He put his arm around her and said, "It's been years, but I'll go to church with you, Noodle."

Darby cried, mumbling under her breath, "If she only knew."

"Knew what?"

"Nothing, Jack, just thinking out loud. I'm glad you're here."

"Me too."

That night, amongst the funeral potatoes, ham, jello and rolls, Jack and Darby Cavanaugh began to get to know each other again.

CHAPTER TEN
The Attic

CLAIRE WAS IN HER ROOM getting ready for bed. She couldn't stand looking at all of the life she had lost. Every trophy and poster took her to a time and place she wished she could go back to; the time before her parents died. The thought of staying in that room made her sadder than before. She took a blanket and left the room.

Wandering down the hall, Claire saw a light in her grandmother's room. It shined brightly on a photograph of her grandmother and mother. The picture sat proudly on the nightstand. She picked it up, held it tight to her chest and curled up on the bed. The pain caused by the death of her parents, felt brand new, as if the accident had just happened.

Claire fell asleep in tears, holding the photograph. Someone walked past her door, but she was asleep and didn't wake up. The light, that seemed to be coming from the moon outside the window, was gone.

A while later, Claire was awakened by a noise. She looked around and saw nothing, so she tried to go back to sleep. When she heard the noise for a second time, she got out of bed to find out where it was coming from.

Claire was not a bit nervous as she walked down the hall of the huge house, past Darby's room, and towards the attic. It was an old house and noises happened. She had been in every nook and cranny of that house at one time or another. Besides, nothing scared Claire. Not even the Reilly attic.

This was one of those attics that you had to walk up a very narrow flight of stairs to get to. Claire got halfway up the stairs and heard the noise again. It stopped her in her tracks, but she slowly moved forward, until she reached the top of the attic stairs. She thought she saw the chair in the corner rocking back and forth, but it stopped when she entered the room. "You need to go back to bed," Claire mumbled to herself. "You're seeing things."

A small dormer window cast a misty light on a huge trunk that sat collecting dust in the corner. It never entered Claire's mind that it was dark outside and there really should be no light shining through the window. She assumed it was the same bright moon she had seen in her grandmother's room.

Claire slowly approached the trunk. She lifted the lid, but closed it, unsure of what she would see. She opened it again and began to look through the trunk. As she looked, she discovered many treasures. She found her grandparents wedding certificate, some old lace linen and a stack of old love letters from John to Kate. A small white box with writing on it appeared from under the letters. She read in a whisper, "Hannah, September 13, 1967 to December 25, 2004."

Claire opened the box and inside she found a tiny white christening gown. She held it up and looked at it. Then pulled it closer, smelled it and rubbed it on her face. It was as if she had found a way to touch her mother.

Moments later, Claire spotted another tiny box. Written on the box was "Madison Jean, August 29, 1958 to November 3, 1958." She slowly opened the box and found a crisp, new christening gown neatly folded inside. She put the lid back on the box and placed it back into the trunk. She didn't want to be disrespectful of this baby that she had never known.

With the christening gowns back in their boxes, Claire spotted an envelope labeled "Family News." She very methodically removed a handful of newspaper articles, and began to read the headlines.

"Claire Lynn Cavanaugh runs off with Blake "Johnny" Johnson."

"Claire Cavanaugh leads cheer team to state finals."

"John Reilly, his daughter, Hannah, and her husband Danny, killed in car crash." That headline stopped Claire cold. She didn't want to read anymore. But not reading the article did not stop her from remembering what happened on that awful Christmas, 12 years earlier.

It was Christmas Eve. Claire was only 17. Her parents, Danny and Hannah, her grandparents, sister and brother were all there. There was a nasty fight between Claire's parents.

Claire's dad was so mad at her grandmother. He kept saying, "This wouldn't be happening if she would mind her own business." Then he slammed out of the house.

"Danny wait," Hannah said, following her husband.

Grandpa kissed Grandma on the forehead and followed Hannah out. He was very protective of his little girl and did not trust Danny one bit. So, he got in the car with Hannah and Danny, and before anyone could stop them, the car sped away.

Claire remembered her grandmother just staring out the window. It was rainy and she let them go. She wouldn't move away from the window. She could have stopped them, but she just stayed at that window. When the police came, she was still standing in the same spot.

"Why didn't you stop them?" Claire said to herself. Then she picked the article up and continued to read. "Danny Cavanaugh, lost control of the car while driving in excess of 100 M.P.H... He had been drinking..."

Claire sat frozen, staring at the yellowing, old newspaper she had never laid eyes on before that moment. Everything she believed, everything she knew to be true was turned upside down in an instant.

The memories of her grandmother paralyzed with fear when the police knocked on the door that night, and the grief she suffered after, returned to Claire's mind. For the first time she realized she had forgotten those moments in order to have someone to blame.

"How did I not know?" She whispered, as tears began to well up inside her.

That night Claire fell asleep, crying again. But this time it was in the attic, amongst old newspapers and an unworn christening gown.

CHAPTER ELEVEN
Nine Years, Seven Months and Two Days

THE NEXT DAY, as promised, Jack accompanied Darby to church. It was not a large church by anyone's standards. But the pews were full and the people seemed genuinely happy to be there.

It was good to be among friends during their time of grief, especially for Darby, who Grandma had raised after her parents died.

The pastor talked about Kate Reilly as if she were a saint.

According to Pastor Jonathon, Kate had helped nearly every person in town at one time or another. Extending credit in the store to people she knew could not pay her back.

"When our own Donald Moore lost his crop," Pastor Jonathon recounted. "Kate Reilly gave him enough seed on credit to start over. She also anonymously donated the church organ." The congregation chuckled when he concluded with, "I guess it's not so anonymous anymore."

Darby was aware of all of this, but Jack had no idea. People sitting near Jack and Darby patted them on their backs, as if to give a big 'amen' to every kind word Pastor Jonathon had said about Kate Reilly.

As they left the church, people stopped to talk with Darby and Jack, to thank them and let them know that all their prayers were with Kate Reilly at this time. Each person had a quick story about how their grandmother helped them in a time of need.

One elderly woman, Mrs. Parker, hobbling behind a walker, stepped forward and gave Darby a big hug. "Hello Darling," she said. "My prayers are with your family."

"Thank you. It's all been a bit more sudden than we expected," Darby replied.

Darby and Jack were in the middle of listening to Old Man Tate talk about how their grandma paid for new tires on his delivery truck, when Jack spotted Bill Simons standing across the street, furtively watching them. When eye contact was accidentally made, Bill tried to leave.

Before he could get into his car, Jack cried out, frantically waving his arms, "Bill, Bill Simons!"

Bill was not very enthusiastic about the reunion. But

it was too late. He had been spotted. "Darby and Jack Cavanaugh. Good to see you," Bill said unconvincingly.

"How long's it been?" Jack asked.

Bill knew exactly how long it had been. He had gone over the moment hundreds of times in his head. "Nine years, seven months and two days," he said. Then he realized he had said too much, so he quickly corrected himself. "About ten years."

"So what have you been up to?" Jack asked.

"Just working."

"What are you doing now?' Darby asked.

"Uh, computers, real estate –"

There was a lot of small talk, but all Bill could think about was getting out of there. He was uncomfortable and wanted to get back into his truck and drive away. "Look guys, it was great to see you, but I gotta run," he said.

"Sounds like you're busy," Darby said. "Not too busy to come by and say hi to Claire though. I know she'd love to see you."

"Yeah, right."

"Really," Darby replied. "Come on over. She could use a–"

Bill's bitterness could not help but escape his lips. "A what? A laugh? A walk down memory lane?" he asked sarcastically.

"I was going to say a friend. I don't think she's very happy."

"Yeah, I was sorry to hear about the divorce." Bill joked.

"Divorce?" Jack asked.

Both he and Darby were shocked! Claire hadn't said anything about a divorce.

"I'm only in town for a few days on business," Bill explained. "I probably won't have time to come by."

As Bill was weaseling his way back into his truck, Darby stopped him. "Find some time," she said. "I know Claire would love to see you. Especially if what you said about the divorce is true."

"Oh, it's true. Martin told me."

"Kitchen door's always open," Jack said.

"I remember," Bill said, as he drove away.

CHAPTER TWELVE

Johnny

BACK AT HOME, Darby and Jack found themselves in the kitchen again, foraging for food. They didn't say it, but both of them secretly hoped that Bill Simons would find his way through their kitchen door once more.

Darby yelled upstairs, "Claire, come down and get some food!"

"Not hungry!"

"Whatever, Sis," Jack hollered. "Get down here and eat with us! You've got some explaining to do!"

In order to stop the yelling, Claire relented and headed downstairs to the kitchen.

When she walked in, Jack asked, "Where's Johnny?"

"He's in New York. I told you, he had to work."

"I know what you told me, Sis," Jack said. "But we just saw Bill Simons and he said you're divorced."

"Bill Simons, when did you–"

"Not the point," Darby added. "Are you divorced?"

"Yes," Claire said. "I couldn't live one more day with that pretentious man."

"Are you okay?" Jack asked.

"Better, now that everyone knows."

"Better enough to eat?" Darby asked.

"Actually, yes. Getting that out has given me quite the appetite."

While Claire, Darby and Jack continued talking and eating, Bill Simons was driving up and down the street trying to convince himself to go in and see Claire. He was also trying to persuade himself not to go see Claire. *She ran off with your best friend,* he thought. *Why would you want to see her? Why would she want to see you?*

The thought of Claire being unhappy should have given Bill a sense of satisfaction, but it didn't. The truth was that Bill still had feelings for Claire. He slammed on his brakes and parked in front of the Reilly house. After that, it only took about fifteen minutes for him to work up the courage to get out of the car. He walked slowly around the familiar path to the back of the house, and to the kitchen door.

When Bill walked in, he didn't expect to see Claire standing only two feet away. Seeing her stopped him in his tracks. "Claire. Uh, Jack and Darby said I could come by," he stuttered.

Claire didn't answer right away. She was shocked to see Bill Simons walk through the door.

Bill assumed she didn't want to see him. He turned around and started to leave. Apologizing for interrupting the family.

But Claire was happy to see Bill Simons. He was the love of her life. She grabbed his arm. "It's good to see you, Billy," she said.

"Billy, huh? You know you're the only one who could get away with calling me that after I hit puberty?"

For some reason Jack found that funny. So he began to tease. "So how ya been, Billy?" he asked.

"Don't test me, Jacky Boy," he said.

Even though they were acting like school boys, Bill and Jack came to an adult understanding. Neither one of them liked to be called by their nick names. But Bill managed to tolerate it when Claire affectionately called him 'Billy'.

Everyone was laughing and having a good time. The kitchen became messier and messier as the cooking and eating continued.

"Remember when we caught Bradley Harding skinny dipping in the stream behind his house? Claire asked.

"Me, you and Johnny stole his clothes and hung them on the flag pole at the high school." Bill said, laughing.

"Those were good times," Claire said.

Then the front door opened and all Claire could hear was, "Anybody home?"

Claire ran out to the front room as fast as she could. Bill, Darby and Jack followed close behind. They all recognized that voice.

Johnny took one look at Bill and said, "Well that didn't take long, did it, Doll? The ink is hardly dry on the divorce papers."

Bill immediately went into protection mode and Claire told Johnny to go home. But Johnny wasn't budging until he got what he came for. He was married to Claire for nearly ten years and wasn't about to walk away empty handed. Especially since Claire had been supporting him for the past few.

"You need to leave now," Bill said.

"What happens between me and my wife is none of your business," Johnny said.

"Ex-wife, Johnny," Claire reminded.

The quiet turned to a kind of unspoken celebration, until Johnny opened his big mouth again. "You know how I hate it when you call me Johnny, Claire."

"What should she call you?" Bill asked.

"Oh, he goes by Blake now," Claire explained.

Bill snickered. He always knew Johnny had a pretentious side. He let it go because they had been best friends. But that was nearly ten years ago, before Johnny stole his girlfriend. "Seriously?" Bill asked. "Look what you gave up," he said staring at Claire.

"I hope you're not getting any ideas about my wife," Johnny said.

"Ex-wife, Johnny," Bill said.

"It's Blake. And I haven't given anything up, yet."

Jack jumped in, "Looks like now might be a good time."

This banter only served to stir Johnny up. "When you're ready to be reasonable, I'll be at my mother's," he said. "Oh, and Bill," he continued, as he walked out the door, "don't forget who took her from you in the first place."

Claire was mortified that Bill had to see who she left him for. It was obviously not a trade up. "I'm sorry, Billy. He's such an idiot," she said.

"It's getting late. I should probably go anyway," Bill said, hoping Claire would stop him. But Claire was frustrated and tired, so she let Bill Simons walk out the door.

Jack, Claire and Darby continued to talk for quite a

while. They talked about Johnny, now calling himself Blake, and how the marriage never worked. Claire even confessed that it was a mistake to run off with him, just to get away from Grandma. Ten years older, she realized and admitted that she could have handled the entire situation better. Claire was a child when she left home. But she was a woman now. With all the experience and heartache that tends to turn to wisdom.

However, for the first time since she had arrived, Claire was almost happy to be home. Happy and exhausted, "I think I'll sleep pretty well tonight," she said.

"If you don't," Darby said. "I'll be in my room, writing. Come visit."

It was a bit early for bed. But it had been a busy and strenuous day in the Reilly house. So Jack, Darby and Claire each went their own way towards their bedrooms.

CHAPTER THIRTEEN
Grandma's Stories

DARBY CAVANAUGH always wanted to be a writer. She spent many hours listening to her grandma's stories of the old country, with the hopes of one day writing a book about them. She was sitting on her bed, just a short while after everyone had said goodnight, when Claire came to her door and knocked quietly. "Hey, Noodle, can I come in?" she asked.

Darby patted the top of her bed. "Climb up."

Claire climbed up on the bed. She was holding a pile of things she had taken out of the attic. Darby looked at the pile and asked, "What's all this?"

"I was sleeping and I heard a noise and went into the attic to check it out."

"You found Grandma's trunk."

"You've seen it?" Claire asked. "Why didn't you tell

me any of this before?"

"I didn't think you wanted to know. You were always so angry. When you ran away, I figured you didn't want anything to do with us."

"It wasn't you. It was this house...her," Claire explained.

"Look, Claire, I know Grandma was a little crusty. But she was a neat lady. I wish you could have heard some of her stories. Stories of her childhood in Ireland and what she gave up to come to America."

Claire looked at the small white box that held Madison's christening dress

"Maddie died just a couple months after she was born," Darby explained.

Darby continued to tell Claire how Grandma and Grandpa always assumed they would have Maddie Christened when they got here. But when they realized she wasn't going to make it, they had a clergyman, who was with them on the boat, quickly baptize her before she died.

"It nearly killed Grandma, physically and emotionally. She bought the dress after they got to America. Maddie never got to wear it. More than nine years after Maddie died," Darby continued. "Grandma found out she was pregnant again. She considered Mom her miracle from God. She had to have her."

"Is that why she was so hard on Dad? He wasn't good enough for her little miracle?"

"No," Darby said. "He wasn't nice enough to her little miracle. He drank, and when he drank, he got mean. When they left the house that Christmas, he had been drinking."

"Why didn't I know?"

"They were good at pretending," Darby said.

"I know about unkind husbands and pretending," Claire responded.

"I'm sorry you've had such a hard time. But you see Claire, Grandma wasn't good at pretending. She was a stubborn, old Irish woman, who was willing to do anything to protect her family."

"I blamed her for everything," Claire cried. "I told her I hated her."

Darby grabbed a tissue from a flowered box on her nightstand and handed it to Claire. "She knew you didn't mean what you said."

"But I did mean it. I ran away with Johnny. I had to get out of this house and I never saw her again."

It seems to me that you got the short end of the stick on that one," Darby said. "Besides, Grandma was a survivor. There was a lot more to her than anyone knew."

"When I was twelve," Darby continued. "I decided I wanted to be a writer. So I started recording Grandma's stories. She was a hoot."

"Do you have any I can listen to?"

Darby hopped off the bed and went to her closet. She grabbed an old shoe box from the top shelf. She removed a tape marked *Grandma's Stories: Tape 1* and put it in an old recorder she had on her nightstand.

Claire laughed, "That recorder is ancient."

"I know. It was Grandma's. I can't get rid of it," Darby said. "Where else can I play all of these old tapes?"

Then she hopped back up on the bed and put the recorder between them. When she pushed the button, Claire heard her grandmother's voice for the first time in many years.

From the hallway, Jack also heard his grandma's voice, so he ran to Darby's room. He peeked inside and saw Darby and Claire all cozy on the bed. "Hey, what are you guys doing? And what's with the old tape recorder?" he asked.

"Shhh," Claire said, patting the bed. "Hop up."

Jack climbed up on the bed with his sisters. They sat mesmerized, staring at the tiny tape recorder that was placed in the middle of the bed.

Grandma's voice filled the air, transporting the siblings to another time and place. She told the story of a tiny five year-old Kate, running out of the house with a

Daisy BB gun tucked under her arm.

I ran into the outhouse and stood on the toilet. Through a hole in the outhouse wall I could see my seven year-old brother, Patrick, collecting eggs in the hen house, a few yards away.

I'm not sure how, but I managed to maneuver the BB gun into the small hole. I aimed, and pretended to shoot at Patrick. The gun accidentally went off and knocked me clean off the toilet seat. The BB hit Patrick in the backside. He dropped the eggs, grabbed his rump and ran crying into the house.

By the time the crying and screaming were over, we'd lost nearly a dozen eggs and I got the whipping of my life. Da took the BB gun and put it up high where only Patrick could reach it.

Jack, Claire and Darby were rolling around on the bed laughing, picturing their grandma shooting their great uncle Patrick in the backside with a BB. "Now I know why I didn't get that Red Rider I wanted for Christmas," Jack chuckled.

"Sins of the father," Claire said. "Or in this case, sins of the grandmother."

"Grandma had a million stories," Darby said.

Claire and Jack begged Darby to play another, and so she did.

Again, Grandma's voice permeated the air.

When we left Ireland, your grandpa's parents gave us twenty dollars, some Irish crystal and china. Family heirlooms. Grandpa promised that no matter what, he would never sell them. He worked very hard to make sure he was able to keep that promise.

Even in our worst times, those precious gifts we got from our parents never left the china cabinet.

Claire and Jack sat with Darby long into the night, listening to stories. It was as if they were trying desperately to get to know the grandmother they had left behind; but no one more than Claire.

CHAPTER FOURTEEN
The Will

THE NEXT MORNING, Martin, Claire, Jack and Darby gathered in the library. A makeshift projector screen was set up at the front of the room. It was finally time for the reading of Grandma's Will.

"Seriously," Jack said. "A projector. Haven't you guys heard of a computer? Between that and the 30 year old tape recorder–"

"Grandma wasn't much for technology," Darby said.

"Obviously," Jack continued.

Martin surveyed the group, and was about to begin when Johnny walked into the room, wearing cream colored linen pants, a pink polo shirt and a blue knitted sweater draped around his shoulders. He looked every bit the part of the wannabe actor he was. "Am I too late?" he asked.

"What are you doing here?" Claire asked.

"Moral support, Love."

"Does he have to be here?" Claire asked.

Martin explained that Johnny didn't have to be there, since they were no longer legally married. But he thought it would be good for Johnny to hear what he had to say. So Claire relented; but not before warning Johnny that if he so much as made a sound, he would be escorted out.

Martin began the speech he had been working on for weeks, "You're grandmother prepared a short message for you."

Martin started the projector and a picture of Grandma came up on a large screen. Claire grabbed Darby's hand. She was shocked at how this reunion was uncovering things she thought she wanted left buried.

"I'm sure that this is completely unnecessary," Martin continued, looking directly at Johnny. "However, I was given strict instructions that if any of you start trouble regarding your grandmother's wishes, you will get nothing."

No one in the room was more interested in what was about to transpire than Johnny. He watched with anticipation, as Martin began the projector.

Grandma began to talk. "I guess it's official. I'm dead."

Martin and Darby chuckled at Grandma's humor, while Jack and Claire did not find it funny.

"Welcome home, Jack," Grandma started. "You were a wild boy, reminded me of my brother Patrick. I never had boys. When your parents and your grandpa died, I didn't know what to do with you. So you were kind of lost in the shuffle. I'm sure your sisters miss you. Come on back home."

Darby looked pleadingly at Jack. "I can't, I have to work," he said.

Grandma continued, "I know you lost your job last fall, Jack."

Jack was shocked that Grandma was aware he lost his job. So Martin paused the projector to explain. He told the kids that their grandmother never stopped worrying about them. Like every other parent, she knew what was going on in their lives. She knew about Jack's job, and Claire's divorce, because that's how caring parents are. And no one cared more about the Cavanaugh kids than Kate Reilly.

When Martin pressed the button, Grandma's voice continued to speak to Jack. "You remember Mr. Connor from Connor Advertising. A couple of years ago they relocated to the top floor of Reilly Inc. Mr. Connor will see you there first thing in the morning for an interview. I told him your computer graphics skills are as good as it gets. Don't make a liar out of me."

"But I don't have my resume or portfolio or –"

"He already has a copy of your resume, and he's willing to give you more money than you were making driving the truck. That way you can stay with your family. If you want the job, it's yours." Grandma said. "But only if it's what you want. Martin's firm will be handling the estate. I won't go into that now, he knows what to do."

Martin paused the VCR, so the offer could sink in and Darby and Claire could rile Jack for not telling them he lost his job. When the commotion was over, Martin resumed the projection and Grandma's voice filled the air once again. "Darby, our little Noodle. Do you know why we always called you Noodle? It wasn't just because you were so skinny, and bendy. It was because you were always thinking, using your noodle, as it were. I know you sacrificed your schooling to stay with me –"

"It was no sacrifice." Darby whispered.

"I sent your transcripts and some of your writing samples to a University," Grandma continued. "They are very well known for their writing program. They want you."

Martin handed Darby a letter with a University letterhead. She opened the envelope. Inside was a letter telling Darby she had been accepted into the creative writing program at Northeastern University. It should have been no surprise to Darby that she was offered a scholarship. She was a straight 'A' student and had been entering writing contests since she was fifteen years-old. But it was a shock. A great big shock. Even bigger when she realized she would have to be ready to go at the start of the very next semester.

Grandma added, "It's amazing what a few well-placed phone calls, not to mention a lot of talent and brains, can do. You have two months to get reacquainted with Jack and Claire before you leave."

Darby began to think of reasons not to go, but Grandma knew her well, and before she could voice any of them, Grandma spoke her final words to Darby. "No excuses child, God willing, your brother and sister will be here when you come home on break."

The realization hit Darby, and it hit her full force. "I guess I'm going to college," she said. "I'M GOING TO COLLEGE!"

After Darby got control of herself, Martin started the projector for one last time. "Hi Claire," she said. "I'm glad you came. I saved you for last because I think I was hardest on you. I couldn't bear the thought of losing another one of my girls. I know I drove you away. I also know you have no reason to go back to New York. Stay here with the people who love you. Darby will need someone to help run the mill while she's gone."

Claire was confused. She was a corporate lawyer. She knew less than nothing about running a mill. She wanted to start her own law firm, not play in sawdust. But Grandma knew all of Claire's wishes and let her know that Martin needed a partner and would love for her to take over the law firm when he retired. Martin seconded Grandma's notion, which they had previously discussed at length.

Up until now, Johnny had sat without saying a word. But the only real reason he was in there was to see if Claire would get something that he might have access to. "What about the money?" he asked.

Claire's anger and frustration with Johnny was palpable. Before she had a chance to start yelling. Martin interrupted. "Now comes the hard part," he said. "Your grandmother had some problems with the business."

"What kind of problems?" Johnny asked.

Claire was done. "Why don't you go wait outside?"

Martin explained that when the economy went south, Grandma signed a very large note and the money was due. Seven years had passed and the lender wanted his money. The bottom-line was that if the business didn't show a nearly impossible profit by the first of the year, no bank would take on the note and everything would be gone.

Johnny couldn't help himself. "Gone?" he asked.

"Yes, Johnny, gone." Martin answered. "May I please

finish now?"

Johnny nodded and Martin continued. "There is a company that wants to buy the business from the bank. If they can, they'll take ownership next week. Condos."

"Who is this so called lender?" Johnny asked.

"I'm afraid that's confidential," Martin said.

"So there is no money?" Johnny asked.

"There's more to it than the inheritance," Martin said.

Johnny got up out of his seat. "What else is there" he bellowed, before storming out of the room.

With Johnny out of the library, Martin continued, "When the business is sold, the house and all of the outstanding notes go with it."

"What notes?" Jack asked.

"I told you Grandma helped a lot of families in town," Darby said.

"Is this what you and Martin were whispering about?" Claire asked.

"Yep, that was it," Darby said. She didn't like to lie, but in this case, she felt that Claire was not ready to know everything yet.

"Why didn't you say anything?" Claire asked.

"Does it matter? It's not about us and our petty garbage. A lot of people, besides us, stand to lose everything."

Martin explained that Reilly Inc. the house and property were in jeopardy. The Cavanaugh children would have to put their differences aside and pull together. Martin had more faith in this family than they had in themselves. But Jack was still confused.

"What does me being a computer 'whiz' have to do with saving the company?"

"Go see Mr. Connor." Martin said. "You'll see."

"I'll take your word for it."

"Please do, and consider everything your grandmother said. If you still need answers, I suggest you check the attic. Spend some time among your grandmother's things. Get to know her."

"I've been there," Claire said.

"Go back," Martin added. "It will help you decide. And Claire – If you're still not sure, you can always pray."

"I don't see that happening any time soon, but thanks for the advice."

Martin's phone rang. He pulled it out of his pocket to see who was calling. The name Bill Simons showed up brightly on the screen. Before Martin could hide it, Darby saw the name.

Martin got up to leave. "I gotta take this call. You kids just stick together and everything will work out," he said.

Darby followed Martin out.

"Where you off to?" Jack asked.

"Little girl's room. We're done here, right?"

"I guess so."

"Then I'll meet you in the kitchen. All this money business is making me hungry."

CHAPTER FIFTEEN
Miracles

THE NEWS ABOUT the Reilly business had confused the kids. There was a lot to think and talk about. The best room in the house for that type of a meeting was the kitchen. Rummaging through the fridge, they ate while they chatted.

Darby was happy to have her sister and brother there to talk to. It felt so good that she didn't even want to think about leaving. "I'm not sure I want to go to school, now that you guys are home," she said.

"You have to go. You're finally going to use that noodle the way God intended," Jack said. "Sorry, Claire. I didn't mean to bring God into the conversation. He obviously had nothing to do with any of the little miracles happening around us."

"What miracles," Claire exclaimed. "All I see is that the family is about to lose everything they ever worked for."

"What about Jack's job, your job, and my school?" Darby asked.

"Reunions, us, you and Bill, all good, huh?" Jack added.

Then another miracle happened. Claire had a moment of realization. "I got your thinly veiled message," she said. "If I blame God for the bad, I've got to give Him credit for the good. I'm a little out of practice."

Darby shoved a piece of chocolate cake into her mouth. "So, are you guys staying?" she asked.

"This has been quite a weekend," Jack said. "And I've got nothing keeping me in LA right now."

"Stop stalling, Jack Cavanaugh," Darby said. "Are you staying or what?"

"I guess I have to stay," he answered. "If for no other reason than to find out what glowing exaggerations Grandma told Mr. Connors."

With Jack on board, Darby began to concentrate on Claire, "What about you, Sis?"

"I don't know. I've got a lot to think about."

"What's to think about?" Jack asked.

"Yeah, what's to think about?" Darby asked.

"It's time to let go of the past," Jack said.

Johnny stomped into the kitchen and announced, "I'll be heading back to New York." Then he left the room.

After the shock and surprise and laughter faded, Jack looked at Claire and said, "Now, that's a miracle."

With Johnny out of the picture, Claire declared, "I think I'm staying."

"We've got her now, Bro," Darby said to Jack.

"I do believe 'The Blakester' has just given us back our sister," Jack replied.

Claire smacked Jack and started to walk out of the room. "Where you going?" he asked. "We're just teasing. You know you want to stay. I'll even cook for you."

"Is that a threat?"

"I can cook, you know," Jack said. "You can't live in LA without being able to whip up a mean pasta."

"Bravo, you can cook spaghetti," Claire laughed.

"That's what I said, pasta."

"Really, Jack," Darby said, "Pasta is just spaghetti with attitude, kind of like you. Besides Claire, if you're scared, I'm a great cook. Grandma taught me all of her recipes."

"If your pancakes are any indication of how you cook, we'll let you do all of the cooking," Claire said.

"Deal," Darby replied. "If that'll keep you from leaving, I'm all in."

"Leave? I can barely leave the kitchen," Jack added.

Darby, barely able to repress her smile, looked around

at the scene that was unfolding. "Grandma would have loved this. 'You miss the good stuff if you stay out of the kitchen,' she always said."

"Judging by the past couple days," Claire said, "I would have to agree with her."

"See, another miracle," Darby teased. "Claire agreed with Grandma."

Claire, Darby and Jack spent the next hour or so reminiscing, eating and laughing. For the first time since she returned home, Claire was having a genuinely good time. As it turned out, the kitchen really was where most of the good stuff happened.

CHAPTER SIXTEEN
Reilly Inc.

LATER THAT DAY, Claire and Jack decided to visit the family business. Reilly Inc. was the biggest building in town. Half of the town owed their living to the giant general store and saw mill, and the other half owed them outright.

"A lot's changed in ten years," Claire said.

"Nine years, seven months and two days." Jack said. "That's how long it's been since the day you left, according to Bill."

"What?"

"So are you going to stay this time?" Jack asked. "Because I'm afraid I'll have to hunt you down if you leave again."

"Really? That's not much of a threat from where I'm standing."

"So I can put away my secret decoder ring?"

"I'm just not sure I can stay here." Claire said.

Jack put his arm around her. "Let's just put our heads together and see if we can figure this out. There's no reason to run from Grandma anymore –"

"Wait a minute, are you playing detective now?" Claire asked.

"I guess I'm not quite ready to give up the decoder ring after all." Jack continued, "You're not running from me or Darby. Maybe, Bill?"

"Don't be ridiculous," Claire protested.

"Or maybe, you're running to something. I've got it! You're not over Johnny. Excuse me, Blake."

"When you put it that way, I guess I really don't have anything waiting for me back in New York."

"Does this mean you're staying?"

"Maybe for a couple weeks."

Jack took Claire's hand and walked towards the large building. "It's a start," he said. "Now let's go inside and see if we can find you an office."

CHAPTER SEVENTEEN
Mom's Trunk

A LITTLE WHILE LATER Jack and Claire were back at home. They entered the kitchen through the back door. Darby was at the counter eating. "Still eating?" Claire asked. "You haven't moved since we left."

"Shows how much you know," Darby said. "That was lunch, this is dinner. You've been gone for over four hours."

Jack and Claire had no idea they had been gone for so long. Their walk down memory lane had lasted for the better part of the day.

"No wonder I'm starving," Claire said. "Jack, how about you whip up some of that famous pasta you keep bragging about."

Jack opened the fridge and started rummaging through the mountain of food. "I would – but there's still some of Darby's spaghetti. It'll be a week before I need to strap on an apron."

"You guys okay here?" Darby asked. "I'm beat and I have a lot to do. I think I'll head upstairs."

Jack and Claire opted to stay in the kitchen and graze for a while. They continued their conversation from earlier. It was as if they had never been apart.

"Thanks for the free therapy, Jack," Claire said.

"Who said it was free. You'll be getting my bill in the mail."

"And you'll be getting my check the same way."

"So you're staying for good?" Jack asked.

"I believe you just informed me that I have no life."

Jack and Claire pushed each other to be first to get through the kitchen door. Jack ran upstairs with Claire chasing after him. They stopped in Darby's doorway. Darby was listening to tapes and writing. "She's staying," Jack said.

"Are you listening to Grandma?" Claire asked.

Darby invited Jack and Claire to listen to more stories. They hopped up on the bed like little kids at a slumber party. Darby took her headphones off and Grandma's voice continued.

That was my best Christmas, until –

At that moment, a loud noise coming from down the

hall startled Darby and she stopped the tape.

Claire recognized the noise. "That's the same noise I heard the other night," she explained. "It's coming from the attic. I think there's something living in there. I'm sure it was watching me before."

"Why didn't you say anything?" Jack asked.

"I guess I was so bothered by what I found, I didn't think about it."

"Martin did say to check out the attic if we wanted to get to know Grandma," Jack added.

They all ran down the hall like they were on a scavenger hunt. They stopped at the top of the attic stairs and Jack slowly went inside. "Did you hear that?" he asked.

The girls didn't hear anything. Jack pushed Darby and Claire into the room in front of him. There was a white dress lying over a rocking chair. He took the dress off the chair and threw it at Claire. "Whooooo... It's the ghost dress," he moaned.

The girls screamed. Darby smacked Jack and took the dress from Claire. "Hey, this is Mom's wedding dress. Where did you get it?" she asked.

"It was on the rocking chair," Jack answered.

"That dress wasn't there a couple of nights ago," Claire said.

"This is our mother's dress," Darby said. "Grandma

showed it to me, hoping that one of us would wear it someday. She was sure that you and Bill would be married and you would wear it."

That made Claire sad.

"But the dress was in her trunk, wrapped in tissue," Darby said.

"Then how did it get here?" Claire asked.

"Grandma said sometimes Mom would come by to check on things," Darby said.

"Oh come on, Sis–where's that noodle of yours when you need it?" Jack asked.

It really didn't matter what Darby said, Jack was a skeptic.

"Grandma used to talk to Mom," Darby replied.

"Just because Grandma talked to her, doesn't mean she was actually there," Jack said.

Claire was less skeptical. "I don't know Jack, I saw the chair rocking by itself when I was here the other night." She remembered feeling the energy that engulfed the room when she was searching through Grandma's trunk. And now she was staring at another trunk. "What's this?"

"That's our Mom's trunk," Darby said. "Let's look inside."

Darby, Claire and Jack gathered around their mother's trunk and started randomly pulling things out. It was clear that their mom must have kept every fruity cereal macaroni necklace and homemade ornament the Cavanaugh kids ever gave her. There were red and green paper chain garlands; macaroni picture frames from each child, complete with a school picture inside; clay handprints; homemade cards; and enough loose glitter to fill a snow globe.

Jack pulled a strand of cranberries with noodles out of the trunk, wrapped it around his neck and declared, "I've heard, one man's junk is another man's treasure."

Darby grabbed the strand from Jack. "Are you kidding, this is treasure," she proclaimed.

"I agree," Claire said. "But how is all this old stuff going to help us get to know our grandmother?"

Darby already knew what was in the trunk, so she convinced Claire to keep looking. Claire found a book and started skimming through it. It was her mom's diary. "Did you know Mom kept a diary?" she asked.

"Grandma started her on it when she was twelve," Darby said. "She got me one when I was the same age. Personal history was very important to Grandma. That's what made me want to become a writer."

"Oh yeah," Claire said. "I vaguely remember Grandma giving me a journal. I used it as a doodle pad."

Jack chimed in. "On my twelfth birthday, Grandma came into my room and gave me a speech on the importance of keeping a personal record of my life. I've always tried to write in it once a week or so."

"I guess I was the only rebellious one," Claire said.

"Let's just say, independent, at a very young age." Jack replied.

Claire began to read out loud from her mother's journal. *"December 24, 2004. I spoke with Mom this morning. She said she would support whatever decision I make. I'm worried about the kids, especially Claire, she loves her dad so much. Mom says she'll be fine. Kids are resilient. I'll tell him after Christmas."*

That was the last entry in the journal. Claire and Jack were confused, they had no idea what the last entry meant. "Tell who, what?" they asked.

Darby explained that their mom was going to ask their dad to leave. The only reason he was still living at the house that Christmas was because of Grandma's Christmas wish. She wanted one more Christmas with the whole family together. "Unfortunately, Dad saw the journal," Darby continued, "and that's what started the argument."

Claire's memories of what had happened that night were contradictory to what really happened. "I distinctly remember Grandma making Dad mad," Claire said.

"Dad was already mad," Darby explained. "When he stormed out that Christmas Eve, it was the last straw. Mom was going to tell him not to come back. She followed him out to the car and Grandpa went with them to protect his little girl."

Now, Claire was even more confused. "Why did Grandma let me stay so mad at her?" she asked.

"Grandma knew Dad was your hero. She was willing to take the blame to keep you from finding out that your father was not the man you thought he was."

"What about me?" Jack asked. "Why didn't anyone tell me?"

"I'm telling you now," Darby said. "Besides, would it have changed anything?"

"Yeah... Maybe," Claire said.

"I probably would have found my way back here more," Jack said.

Finally, the realization that her grandma was not at fault hit Claire. "My gosh Darby," she said. "I blamed her and now it's too late to do anything about it!"

"What would you have done?" Darby asked. "Not runaway? Stayed here and made babies with Bill? What?"

First, she felt guilty about Grandma and soon Claire realized what she had done to Bill. It was almost too much for her to bear. "I really hurt Billy," she said. "And Grandma–she must have thought I was awful."

"Never. She always loved all of us," Darby said.

"That's why it's so important for all of us to be here now."

"That's great," Jack said. "She finally gets her Christmas wish and she's not here to enjoy it."

"I'm sure she's here in spirit," Darby said.

"Yeah, yeah, she's standing in the corner with Mom, I see her," Jack replied sarcastically.

After all of the revelations and the tears were shed in the attic, the kids decided to grant Grandma her wish. The wish that was shattered on Christmas Eve, almost 12 years ago. The family would be together this Christmas, no matter what.

"Jack, what if we meet you at the cemetery after your interview with Mr. Connor tomorrow," Claire said. "At least if Grandma can't be with us, we can be with her.

"Sounds great," Jack said.

"How does the story end?" Claire asked Darby

"What story?"

"Grandma said that was her best Christmas ever until – Until what?"

"Oh yeah, it was, 'her best Christmas ever, until she had kids of her own to share them with.'"

CHAPTER EIGHTEEN
Mr. Connor

THE NEXT MORNING, Darby was in the kitchen making breakfast. It was the day of Jack's meeting with Mr. Connor, and she wanted to make sure he ate a healthy breakfast before he left the house.

"Come and get it, lazy bones," Darby hollered up the stairs. "You're going to be late."

Jack came bounding into the kitchen, battling with his tie. "I hate these things," he said. "I never understood why wearing a tie was necessary for getting a job."

Then he looked up at Darby in her apron, cooking as if she'd been cooking forever. "Look at you being all domesticated."

"Watch it, mister," Darby said, wielding a stainless steel spatula. "I'm your worst nightmare with a kitchen utensil."

"I believe you," Jack said, trying to escape Darby's reach.

Jack and Darby were chasing each other around the kitchen when Claire walked in. "You eating without me?" she asked.

"Got to, if we want to eat at all," Jack said. "The way you've been packing it in, since you've decided to eat."

"You're hysterical," Claire said. "Aren't you late for an interview or something?"

Jack stuffed a piece of toast in his mouth and left reluctantly through the kitchen door, with a last longing look at a counter-full of food.

So much for a healthy breakfast!

"That's it?" Darby protested. "One piece of toast?"

But Jack was already out the door.

~~~~~~~

FOR THE SECOND TIME in two days, Jack found himself at Reilly Inc.

If at all possible, he wanted to help the company.

Mr. Connor sat across the desk from Jack. "We can't pay big city advertising wages, but you will have complete creative control in whatever you do. And your main account will be Reilly Inc.," he said.

"Oh, now I get it," Jack said, sounding a bit perturbed. "In exchange for the Reilly accounts, you have to hire me."

"We already have the Reilly accounts," Mr. Connor explained. "They are failing miserably. That's why we need you. You have Reilly blood and I believe you will bring a fresh new approach to the business. Besides," he concluded, "your grandmother mentioned what a great graphic artist you are. You could be just what both our businesses need."

"I'll do it, but I need to start quickly," Jack said. "I owe it to my family."

"Is now soon enough?" My Connor said with a grin.

~~~~~~~

WHILE JACK WAS at his interview, Claire decided to take a walk back to the greenhouse to think.

A lot had happened since she had returned to her hometown. She wandered past the basil, then snipped a piece of lemon thyme and put it in her mouth. As she stood there savoring the bright lemon flavor, Bill walked in and made her jump. No one ever entered the greenhouse without warning while Claire was deep in thought.

Bill apologized for scaring Claire. He only wanted to

talk to her. He asked her if he could take her out for coffee. She didn't drink coffee. It gave her energy she didn't want or need. In fact, Claire's normal energy level made gnats nervous.

"Tea, soda, or maybe just a talk?" Bill asked.

"Darby and I are meeting Jack at the cemetery. But I can go when we get back."

"Sounds great."

Bill and Claire walked out of the greenhouse together, passed the horses, grazing in the grass; and passed the chickens gossiping in the coop. As a matter of fact, Claire and Bill were so engrossed in each other that they didn't see Darby sitting by the pond with her feet dangling in the cool blue water; so wrapped up in writing her stories that she didn't see them walk by from across the field.

CHAPTER NINETEEN
The Cemetery

JACK WALKED AS QUICKLY AS HE COULD to his grandma's grave. It was still a mound of dirt with some wilted flowers lying around from the funeral. Darby and Claire were already there.

"Sorry I'm late," Jack said. "You're looking at the new Creative Consultant for Connor Advertising. My first job is to come up with a fresh new look for Reilly Inc. That means I'll be spending lots of time with you, Claire."

At last, all three of the grandkids stood together around their grandma's grave. It would have been a joyous occasion had Grandma lived to see it. Each of the kids spent a moment talking with Grandma.

Apologies were made and more tears were shed. Jack and Claire came to know their grandma a little better through Darby's stories. "You know," Darby said. "Grandma was really the driving force behind Reilly Inc.

but she gave grandpa all the credit."

"How do you know so much about grandma?" Claire asked.

"I spent a lot of time in the kitchen," she replied.

"I've learned more in a couple of days in the kitchen than in four years of college," Jack said. "Maybe we should continue this conversation at home, in the kitchen."

"I'll have to catch up with you later," Claire said. "I have to run a quick errand after this."

When they left the cemetery, they were so engrossed in their day that they didn't see the large black limousine come and go.

~~~~~~

MARY'S DINER SERVED the best berry pie in town, and it had been a long time since the deep purple of yummy boysenberries had touched Claire's lips. In fact, the last time she had visited the diner she was with Bill Simons. So it was only right that he be sitting across from her sharing a piece of pie now. That is if sharing meant that Bill got two bites and Claire unapologetically devoured the rest.

They talked for a long time and even though Bill wanted desperately to tell Claire about the loan he had given her grandmother, he couldn't bring himself to do it. Even though, he was having second thoughts.

Claire and Bill sat deep in conversation, while Johnny sat at a stop light in his dark blue, compact rental car. Unfortunately, the stop light was on the same corner as Mary's Diner. As he waited for the light, he found himself looking through the diner window. The light changed just as Johnny spotted Claire and Bill. He put his foot on the gas and screeched through the light.

CHAPTER TWENTY
Claire and Billy

WHEN CLAIRE RETURNED home, Darby and Jack were in the kitchen eating ice cream.

"Come join us," Darby said.

Claire had just eaten most of a very large piece of pie and the thought of eating ice cream didn't sit well with her. But she was reluctant to tell her brother and sister that she had just spent the past hour with Bill Simons. For whatever reason, she had begun to care about what her siblings thought.

"I'm not really hungry," Claire said,

"Please don't start that again," Jack snapped.

"No, no, I just ate," Claire said with pause. "I was at Mary's Diner–with Bill."

"We were wondering where you disappeared to," Darby said.

Truly, this was happy news for everyone. Teasing turned into laughter and laughter led to more memories. Memories that began to work their way back into Claire's heart.

"Remember when Grandma got mad at the paper boy," Jack recounted. "After about the fifth time of having to retrieve the paper from the bushes, she picked it up and threw it right back at him. Knocked him clean off his bike and into the gutter."

"Yeah," Darby continued. "After that, he never missed the porch."

The raucous laughter coming from the Reilly kitchen was dampened and silenced when Johnny came back into the house. "I just wanted to say goodbye," he said. "There's nothing for me here anymore. I'll have my lawyer contact you."

Johnny started to leave the house and Claire stopped him. The past ten years had not been all bad. She actually loved Johnny at one point in time and she didn't want either of them to be bitter. Especially since she was getting her family back. "Wait, Johnny," she said, following him to the front door. "You can have everything. I have no need for it now. Take the house, the furniture, the car, all of it."

Johnny was taken aback. Why would Claire be willing to give him everything? "Everything?" he asked.

"Johnny, I'm sorry things turned out the way they did. I'm learning, I need to think of the good times. And we did have some good times, right?"

Johnny agreed. Right then and there in that big house, amongst all of the valuables, without ever telling Claire he had seen her with Bill, Johnny agreed to go back to New York without her. They wished each other well, and even shared a hug.

Johnny was gone.

CHAPTER TWENTY-ONE
Claire's Prayer

CLAIRE RETURNED TO THE KITCHEN where Jack and Darby admitted they had heard everything. It was bittersweet, for as much as Johnny annoyed them, he had been family.

Claire excused herself and went into her grandma's room. She sat on the bed and picked up the photo of her grandma and mom that sat on the night stand beside the bed. She started to cry, "I miss you, Mama."

Then, something amazing happened. Claire began to pray. "God, it's Claire Johnson. The last time we talked I was Claire Cavanaugh. You probably don't even know who I am anymore. But if you could find a way to let Grandma know I'm sorry –"

Claire's grandmother entered the room without Claire knowing. She stroked Claire's hair and whispered, "I know child."

Claire turned around and there was her grandmother, very much alive. "Grandma," she said. "But you're dead."

"Let's just say the news of my death was a bit premature," Grandma said, losing her balance.

"Are you all right?"

"Just a little heart attack or two. I'll be fine, if I can just get back into my own bed."

"Are you going to get better?"

"I hope so."

Claire helped her grandma back to her own room and into her bed. "Sorry, I've been sleeping in your room."

"It's okay, child."

They talked and talked and Grandma explained everything. There were twenty rooms and many passages in the Reilly house. That made it easy for her to watch everything without being seen. She was watching from the window when Claire and Jack first arrived, and she was on a closed circuit television during the reading of the Will.

"That's why you used the projector set up? I thought you just refused to buy new technology. Darby's tape recorder?"

"That was her choice. She refuses to keep up with the times."

"But why did you fake the funeral?" Claire asked.

Darby walked into the room, kissed her grandma on

the forehead and said, "I'll answer that. Grandma needs to rest."

"You knew?" Claire asked.

"Somebody had to take care of her."

"Why didn't you tell me?"

Darby took Claire by the arm and started to leave her grandma's room. She didn't want to get Grandma upset, but Grandma wanted to explain. She thought it was her responsibility to tell Claire the reason she hadn't told them she was home. "I just wanted the family together for one last Christmas, before I'm gone."

"And I was hoping that if we made it the best Christmas ever, she'd get well," Darby said.

"Did you know about the business and the house?" Claire asked Darby.

"That was news to all of us," Darby said. "I just wanted Grandma to get better."

"I don't think that's going to happen, Noodle," Grandma said.

"Have faith. We're all here now." Claire said. "You'll get better."

Claire's declaration of faith was a wonderful thing to hear. She and Darby vowed that they would make this Grandma's best Christmas ever.

When Jack heard the news that his grandma was alive

and in her room, he ran as fast as he could to see her. The reunion with all three of her grandchildren gave Grandma the kind of hope that she hadn't dared to entertain in years.

CHAPTER TWENTY-TWO
One-Legged Hose

IT WAS CHRISTMAS Eve day. Darby, Jack and Claire met in the attic to find the Christmas decorations.

Darby left Jack and Claire to dig through the old ornaments while she ran out to get some new ones.

At least that was the excuse she gave. Darby actually went to Martin Westerly's office. When she walked in, Bill Simons was just walking out. Darby wanted to talk to Martin about Grandma, but when she saw Bill she decided it was more important to talk with him about Claire. She ran out of the building after him.

Bill didn't want to talk to Darby, but Darby was persistent.

"Johnny went back New York."

Bill kept walking.

"Claire gave him everything. She's staying here."

"That's great," Bill said, as he continued moving

forward.

Darby was trying to reach Bill, so she just starting saying random things. "Grandma's alive. And, it seems there's someone in town who wants the business to fail. Any ideas?"

That caught Bill's attention, but he wasn't sure what to say. "Why would I...?" he asked.

"I don't know, I guess I just wanted you to know."
After a moment, Bill caught himself being sucked back in. Then he stopped abruptly. "Look, I have to go."

"She never stopped thinking about you."

It was obvious that Bill was moved. But he had gotten himself into a situation, he wasn't sure he could get out of. He got into his car and started it up.

"Why did you call Martin the other day?" Darby asked.

"Business. How did you know?"

"I saw your name come up on his phone."

Bill was preoccupied. He was trying to figure out what to do about the business. He had investors ready and a plan set in motion, but he wasn't sure he could go through with it now. "Look, I gotta go."

Before Bill had a chance to drive away, Darby said, "I know Claire had a great time with you at Mary's. The kitchen door's still open."

"I know, I know." Bill said. And he was gone again.

When Darby returned home, Jack and Claire were still in the attic surrounded by boxes.

"About time," Claire said. "Where are the decorations?"

"Oh—I didn't find any I liked. Let's just use what we have."

Darby started rummaging through Christmas boxes. She didn't want to tell Claire she had just seen Bill. "What do we have here?" she asked.

"Oh my goodness," Claire said. "She still has the Christmas mouse! They made these for the church bazaar before you were even born, Noodle."

"Before I was even born," Jack said. "And here's the cardboard picture ornament I made in 3rd grade. Hasn't she ever heard of a white elephant gift? These are prime."

"You know how she was about getting rid of anything?" Darby said. "Potato famine mentality."

"I thought we found the majority of the hoard the other night, but this is amazing!" Jack said. "How come I didn't see any baggies hanging to dry on the kitchen faucet?"

"She hasn't been in the kitchen," Darby answered. "They were prominent at Thanksgiving."

"Do you remember the nylons?" Claire asked.

Evidently, Grandma had amassed a drawer full of one-legged hose. If she got a run in her nylons, she would cut off the affected leg and dispose of it. Since her hose never, ever varied in color, it was easy for her to put on two one-legged pairs without anyone ever suspecting.

"She doesn't still do that?" Claire asked. "Does she?"

"Yep," Darby said. "Lives in a mansion and cuts the bad leg off a pair of nylons. She's probably wearing two one legged pairs of nude, sheer toe hose right now."

Claire, Jack and Darby sat looking through boxes of memories, telling stories and laughing, and the years quickly melted away.

"I'm so glad you guys are here," Darby said. "Hey, how about we go get some breakfast?"

"Breakfast, this is lunch," Claire said. "While you were out looking for the perfect non-existent Christmas decorations, we ate breakfast. Where did you go anyway?"

Darby quickly changed the subject. "No wonder I'm starved," she said. "Race you."

Covered in glitter, they all ran down the stairs, and into the kitchen. But this time Claire was racing, and she made it clear to everyone that she was the winner. "I won!" She said. "Hey, we'd better hit the sink. You know how Grandma hates messes."

"Do you think we can keep her upstairs all day?"

Darby asked.

"No problem. I'll handle it," Claire said.

"We can take turns visiting and catching up with her." Jack said. "I'm sure between the two of us we have enough to talk about to keep her down for the day."

"If you guys want to record some stories for my book while you're up there, that would be awesome," Darby said.

With Grandma home, a feast was in order. Darby would be busy running the kitchen with the help of whichever sibling wasn't with Grandma. It was going to be her best Christmas ever.

Claire started the vigil. She took Grandma a beautiful meal, prepared with love.

When she entered the room, Grandma looked up and said, "Claire, you are here. I was afraid I was dreaming. Stinking medication makes me loopy."

Claire placed the tray on her grandma's bed and sat beside her. "I brought you something to eat," she said.

It was a tender moment and Grandma wanted to say the right things. She knew that Claire had been holding the photo from the nightstand. She had watched her crying a few nights earlier.

Grandma pointed to the photograph and said, "I talk to her sometimes. I could swear she came to get me last week. I told her to go back and send my John or I wasn't going anywhere."

"I guess she got the message," Claire said. "You're still here. Besides, you can't leave yet."

"That's what I heard."

"Grandma, I'm sorry," Claire said.

"Not another word, child."

Claire helped Grandma eat. At the time, it seemed like the only way to let her know how sorry she was.

They could hear Jack and Darby singing Christmas carols downstairs. It made Grandma smile, just knowing her whole family was together.

"Here's the deal," Claire said. "I'll go see what all the noise is about, while you try to take a short nap."

Claire tucked her grandma in and hugged her tight. Grandma hugged her back. At that moment, years of sadness, anger and upset gave way to gentle tears, and the eventual soft breathing that comes with contentment.

CHAPTER TWENTY-THREE
The Feast

JACK AND DARBY were busy cooking, singing *Jingle Bells* and generally bossing each other around. Jack was wearing a Santa hat and Christmas apron adorned with all manner of holly and lace, while Darby donned reindeer antlers and Santa slippers.

In the middle of making stuffing, Jack piped up, "Hey Noodle, do you know the name of the horse in *Jingle Bells*?"

"What are you talking about?" Darby asked. "There's no specific horse in *Jingle Bells*."

Jack kept singing, "Bells on Bob's tail ring. His name's Bob, duh."

By now Darby was cracking up. She couldn't decide whether or not she wanted to burst his bubble. Then she announced, "That's bobtails, oh sultan of song."

Jack and Darby kept singing and laughing as they finished preparing for the Christmas feast.

Besides the regular table fare, there were three different kinds of pie. Claire loved berry, Darby was a fan of apple, and Jack and Grandma were suckers for the traditional pumpkin. The smells of Christmas permeated the air with a spirit long absent.

Jack surveyed the food. The prime rib was in the oven, the mashed potatoes and gravy were done, the green beans were on the stove, the ham was resting, and the rolls were rising. Feeling extremely proud of their accomplishments, Jack wanted to leave the mess and finish decorating.

By then, Claire had come into the kitchen to find out what all the noise was, and together, against Darby's better judgment, they decided to leave the disaster behind in the kitchen, and decorate for Grandma. Having helped Jack and Darby reach that conclusion, Claire went back upstairs to shed some more tears with her grandmother.

While she was placing the Baby Jesus in the manger, Darby heard a car pull into the front yard. She looked out the window and could see Bill sitting in his car, talking on the phone. Something wasn't right. It looked to Darby as if he was in an argument. When he hung up the phone, Darby quickly moved away from the window and busied herself with the creche.

Minutes later, when the doorbell rang, Darby knew who it was, but Jack decided to be feisty and fight her to answer the door. When they finally got the door opened, Bill was standing on the front stoop with a very large Christmas tree. "I know you said the kitchen door was always open, but I didn't think this would fit through the back door," he said.

Jack laughed. He hadn't seen a tree that big since his grandpa was alive. "Yep, that's just like the trees Gramps used to bring home. Always too big to fit through the back door," he said.

Then he yelled up the stairs, "Claire, Billy's here!"

Bill still wasn't going to let Jack call him Billy. That name was strictly reserved for Claire. So he gave Jack a nasty look and pushed past him into the living room.

Jack respectfully corrected himself. "Bill's here!" he hollered.

Claire came running down the stairs. When she got close to the bottom, she slowed down to fix her skirt. She took one look at the tree and asked, "What have you done?"

Bill had heard from a little bird that the Cavanaugh trio were going to get a tree later in the day, so he decided to save them the trip. Claire was thrilled, but tried not to act too excited. Then Bill confessed that it wasn't entirely selfless. He was hoping to take Claire for a drive to talk. And, maybe later, wrangle an invitation for dinner.

Jack and Darby thought it would be a great idea for Bill to come to dinner, because he could help with the work; until they realized that not only would Bill not be around to help, he would be taking Claire with him.

"Can you guys spare Claire for a little while?" Bill asked.

The idea of Claire being happy made it easy for Jack to say, "Go on. Get out of here."

And so, they did. But not before Bill let them know how amazing the house smelled, while ensuring his invite to come back for dinner.

CHAPTER TWENTY FOUR
Secrets Revealed

CLAIRE SAT WITH BILL in front of Reilly, Inc. Bill stared at the building. "It would have been a beautiful community," he said. "Only now I can't do it."

"What are you talking about?"

Bill proceeded to tell Claire everything about how he was the real estate developer who was going to buy the business and call in the loans; about how he never thought she'd come back to town, but when she did and he saw her, it felt like his heart would burst.

The domino effect that started with a newspaper in the attic, had mended Claire's relationship with her grandma and brought her to that moment with Bill Simons, the love of her life. She was no longer angry or bitter, she was vulnerable and kind. Finally, she felt worthy to love and be loved.

Bill Simons had been waiting for this moment for nearly a decade–Nine years, seven months and two days–to be exact. Although he tried to deny it, he had never stopped loving Claire. He vowed, right there and then that he never would. And then he kissed her.

~~~~~~

BACK AT THE HOUSE, Jack and Darby were surveying the family room. The decorating was almost complete, when Bill and Claire came back. "Looks great," Claire said.

"Good of you two to show up and help," Jack said.

"So, how was your drive?" Darby asked.

It was apparent that Bill and Claire had a good talk. It was also evident that they were not going to divulge any details. So everyone continued decorating until all that was left was to put the angel on the tree.

Darby carefully unboxed the angel and started quietly humming *"Hark the Herald Angels Sing."* By the time everyone joined in, the singing was much louder and it didn't take long before Grandma was standing in the family room.

Grandma looked around at the happy scene and the wonderful decorations, "What's all this?" she asked.

"You're supposed to be resting," Claire said.

"How can anyone rest with all this commotion?"

"Sorry. We'll be quiet." Jack said.

"Are you kidding, this is the best sound I've heard in years."

Now that Claire was letting the good memories back in, she remembered that Grandma's favorite part of decorating, was placing the angel on the tree. She took the angel from Darby and handed it to Grandma. Then Jack and Bill helped her onto a small step-ladder to place the angel on the top of the tree.

Once the angel was placed, and everyone was standing around the tree, Grandma hit the switch and the entire room was engulfed in light. More light than anyone thought possible.

"Grandma," Darby said. "Go upstairs and rest so you'll have enough energy for the celebration."

"Not happening child. I feel great and I'm not about to miss out on any more of this."

"Do I have to throw you over my shoulder and carry you back upstairs?" Jack asked.

Grandma smacked Jack on the backside. "You've always been a cheeky child," she said.

"Okay, I'll let you stay up if you just sit and watch," Jack said.

Grandma relented and the festivities continued with

her sitting comfortably in her rocking chair. She watched joyfully as the goings on resumed. Jack, Darby, Bill and Claire reminded Grandma of an ant colony, following each other from place to place with different items in their hands, making ready for the feast. Somewhere between butter and green beans, she fell asleep.

CHAPTER TWENTY FIVE
Chocolate Covered Cherries

THE TABLE WAS set for dinner, Grandma was asleep in her rocking chair, and the doorbell rang.

Jack and Darby fought over who would answer it. Only this time, it wasn't about who got to answer it, but who had to answer it. Rather than listening to the juveniles, Bill and Claire answered the door.

A group of carolers were standing on the porch singing. *"We Wish you a Merry Christmas"* echoed throughout the Reilly house.

The carolers were ecstatic to see that Grandma was still alive. Each caroler was holding a Christmas card addressed to Kate. Martin Westerly was in the back of the crowd, wearing a Santa hat and holding a box of chocolate covered cherries.

Martin pushed his way to the front of the crowd. "A

little bird told me Santa was here," he said.

"Oh really," Claire said. "That little bird must be having an extremely busy day."

Martin feigned surprise when he saw Bill there, holding Claire's hand. The two men had a bit of a secret, and it was evident that it was a good secret.

Martin walked over to Grandma. She was sleeping, so he placed the box of chocolate covered cherries on her lap and gave her a kiss on the cheek. "Merry Christmas, Kate."

Grandma woke up and looked around. Not only did she have her favorite chocolates sitting on her lap, but she had a house full of friends and neighbors.

One by one they started handing her Christmas cards. Inside each Christmas card was a check. Every person who came to carol that Christmas Eve was relieved that Grandma was alive and every one of them gave all that they could to repay their loans and help her out. No one was able to pay all that they owed. But they gave all that they had.

When the crowd started for the front door, Grandma set the box of chocolates on the end table and walked to the door to say goodbye. When the last caroler had hugged Grandma and wished her well, Martin handed her the box of chocolates and asked her to open it.

But Grandma wanted to wait until after dinner. She

loved chocolate covered cherries and she knew if she ate one, she would eat them all and her appetite would be spoiled. Darby and Jack agreed. They had just spent all day making the perfect feast for Grandma and they wanted her to savor every bite.

Grandma started to put the box aside and Bill got impatient. "Open it!" he said. "I mean, I would love a chocolate covered cherry."

As far as anyone knew, it was just a box of chocolates, but to Bill and Martin it was something else.

"Please open it, Kate," Martin said. "For me."

Grandma could never refuse the man who had been her dearest friend for what seemed like forever, so she opened the box. Sitting on top of the candy was a piece of paper stating that someone, who wished to remain anonymous, had paid her note.

Darby and Claire looked at Bill, who was trying to be inconspicuous, but they knew. Grandma knew as well. She gave Bill a huge hug and let him know that she would still pay him back.

Bill looked at Claire, "If everything goes the way I hope, it'll all be kept in the family," he said.

Grandma was so filled with gratitude that for a moment she was speechless. But only for a moment. She invited Bill and Martin to stay for dinner, without realizing they had already planned on it. It was surprising how Bill Simons and Martin Westerly fit right in at the Reilly house.

Jack was the only one who had no idea what was going on. "I hope during dinner someone will fill me in. I must have missed something," he said.

"Come on Jack," Darby said, pulling him towards the dinner table. "We'll get you caught up."

CHAPTER TWENTY-SIX
Grandma's Christmas Wish

THE FAMILY GATHERED around the dining room table. As always, there was no shortage of food for the annual Christmas feast.

Darby was the only one who seemed to have all of the pieces of the puzzle, so she explained everything to Jack, who refused to eat until he was clued in to the situation.

Content with Darby's explanation, Jack started to take a spoonful of mashed potatoes. Grandma smacked the spoon out of his hand. "Who'd like to give thanks for the food?" she asked.

In true family form, they all avoided eye contact with Grandma. Except for Claire who, much to everyone's surprise, announced that she would like to say the prayer. "I think I owe God a few prayers, she said. "About ten years' worth."

The family held hands, bowed their heads and Claire began, "Dear God, thank you for this food and the loving hands that prepared it–"

Jack let out a rather premature "Amen," before Grandma shushed him.

Claire continued, "And thank you for bringing us all together this Christmas. Oh, and thank you for remembering me. Amen."

After the collective "Amen," Darby asked Grandma if she would tell the story of her mom and the Christmas tree.

Grandma was a bit reluctant until Claire asked, "Please, Grandma. I've really wanted to hear you tell one of your stories in person."

Of course, Grandma could not refuse, and so she began, "This story took place in this very house, when your mother was only two years-old. Every year at Christmas time, your grandpa would go into the woods and cut down the perfect tree. Always too tall, so the top branches would need to be cut in order to fit into the room. He would take the extra branches and nail them to other parts of the tree so it would be perfectly symmetrical–"

Jack laughed. "I remember that. I used to help. We always had the perfect tree."

"We had to cut the top off the monster Bill brought over today, to make sure there was room for the angel,"

Darby added.

Everyone chuckled, then Grandma continued, "Well, this particular year, Grandpa and I were busy in the kitchen, when we heard a cry for help. We rushed into the living room to find your two year-old mother, wearing only a diaper, crying. She had climbed to the top of the Christmas tree and was stuck. While we were trying to get her down, she took matters into her own hands. She began to slide down the trunk of the tree, taking out about a dozen branches on her way down."

The joy and laughter in the room could not be contained. Anyone who was within five miles of the Reilly house could have felt the love coming from within.

Grandma was pleased to see her entire family eating and laughing together on Christmas, it was all she could do to contain the excitement. It was all she ever wished for. All she would continue to wish for as long as she had breath to wish.

CHAPTER TWENTY-SEVEN
Together Again

IT HAD BEEN one year since Jack and Claire had returned home. The house was decorated for another Christmas. Jack, Martin, Bill and Claire, wearing a shiny wedding ring, were gathered around the Christmas tree when the front door opened.

Darby rushed in, calling out, "Anybody home?"

Everyone ran to greet her. The hugs were flying around the room like a helium balloon with a leak.

"Noodle!" Jack shouted.

Darby touched Claire's pregnant belly. "Hello, niece," she said.

"Five more months," Claire added.

"Come in and check out the tree," Bill said, giving Darby a bear hug.

They all went into the family room, where they were met by Grandma, looking much better than the year before.

"I thought I heard you come in," she said.

Darby hugged her grandma for a long time. "Look at you, Grandma, sassy as ever."

"Evidently, Claire has a direct line to God," Grandma said. "I might live forever."

Claire put her arm around Grandma, "I can only hope."

"I have something for you," Darby said. Then she reached into her bag, pulled out a book and handed it to Grandma.

Grandma took the book and read the cover out loud. "Grandma's Christmas Wish?"

"You finished it!" Jack exclaimed.

"You knew about this?" Grandma asked.

"Of course I did. She's been working on it since she was twelve."

Grandma held the book to her chest. "I can't wait to read it. Will you sign it for me?"

"Seriously?" Darby asked.

"I want one too," Claire said.

Darby snickered. "I'm pretty sure I have copies for everyone. Right now they're pretty easy to come by."

"Not for long Noodle," Jack said, "It'll be a best seller in no time."

"Of course it will," Darby said sarcastically.

"Now that Darby's here, we can put the angel on the tree," Grandma said.

"You waited for me. Yay!"

Bill and Jack helped Grandma place the brilliant angel that had adorned the Reilly tree for nearly half a century.

"Ready?" Darby asked, before flipping the switch.

Grandma stood mesmerized at the heavenly host atop the tree. It seemed to shine more brilliantly than ever. So bright that one by one the family began to glance upward. Even the baby Jesus, lying in his manger seemed to be gazing heavenward.

If you ask the Cavanaugh kids what they saw that night, they would swear the entire family was there, gathered above the angel, wishing Grandma a Merry Christmas.

About The Author

Shelley Bingham Husk was born and raised in Southern California, where her love for words began at the age of four.

Her poetry and libretti have been commissioned by the California State PTA; composer Brent Pierce; artist Alan McMurtrey and novelist Michael Jensen.

Shelley recently received the Filmed in Utah Award for her screenplay "The Last Straw" starring Corbin Bernsen.

Shelley currently resides in Utah with her husband Dale, where she continues to write and produce films; is working on books two and three of the "American Apparitions Trilogy" (book one *The Ghost of Little Elm Lake* was released in February); and is on the board of directors for the Park City International Film Festival.